Eddie Ayres grew up in England and has adventured throughout the world as a viola and cello player. After working in an orchestra in Hong Kong, he decided to cycle from England back to Hong Kong (that's 16,000 km), took a little violin with him, and played to Greek shepherds, Iranian police and Chinese truck drivers along the way. For ten years, he worked as a broadcaster with the ABC. Eventually his adventurous spirit demanded more, and he moved to Afghanistan to teach music there for a year. Eddie was born Emma, and transitioned just before his fiftieth birthday.

Ronak Taher is an award-winning Iranian-Australian filmmaker and visual artist based in Melbourne, Australia. She obtained a Bachelors in Visual Art from Tehran University of Art in Iran, where she discovered her mission and vision as a contemporary storyteller who uses different mediums. In 2017, she completed her Masters in Film and Television at Victorian College of the Arts, Melbourne University. Ronak's artwork is installed in Melbourne suburbs as light boxes and wall murals and her films and animations have screened in film festivals around the world. She has illustrated picture books in Iran, Australia and France.

SONAM
and the SILENCE

To Charlie. Ease, joy and glory. ⌒ EA

For all kids experiencing war
who will never have a chance to
read this book. ⌒ RT

Published by Allen & Unwin in 2018

Text copyright © Eddie Ayres 2018
Illustrations copyright © Ronak Taher 2018

Allen & Unwin
83 Alexander Street
Crows Nest NSW 2065
Australia
Phone: (61 2) 8425 0100
Email: info@allenandunwin.com
Web: www.allenandunwin.com

Allen & Unwin – UK
Ormond House, 26–27 Boswell Street,
London WC1N 3JZ, UK
Phone: +44 (0) 20 8785 5995
Email: info@murdochbooks.co.uk
Web: www.murdochbooks.co.uk

A catalogue record for this book is available from the National Library of Australia
catalogue.nla.gov.au

A catalogue record for this book is available from the British Library.

ISBN (AUS) 978 1 76029 366 6
ISBN (UK) 978 1 76063 487 2

For teaching resources, explore www.allenandunwin.com/resources/for-teachers

Cover and internal design by Kirby Armstrong
Author photograph by Russell Shakespeare
Set in 19 pt Appareo
Colour reproduction by Splitting Image, Clayton, Victoria

This book was printed in March 2018 at Shenzhen Wing King Tong Paper Products Co., Ltd. Shenzhen, Guangdong, China.

10 9 8 7 6 5 4 3 2 1

SONAM
and the SILENCE

EDDIE AYRES

Illustrated by RONAK TAHER

ALLEN&UNWIN

SYDNEY · MELBOURNE · AUCKLAND · LONDON

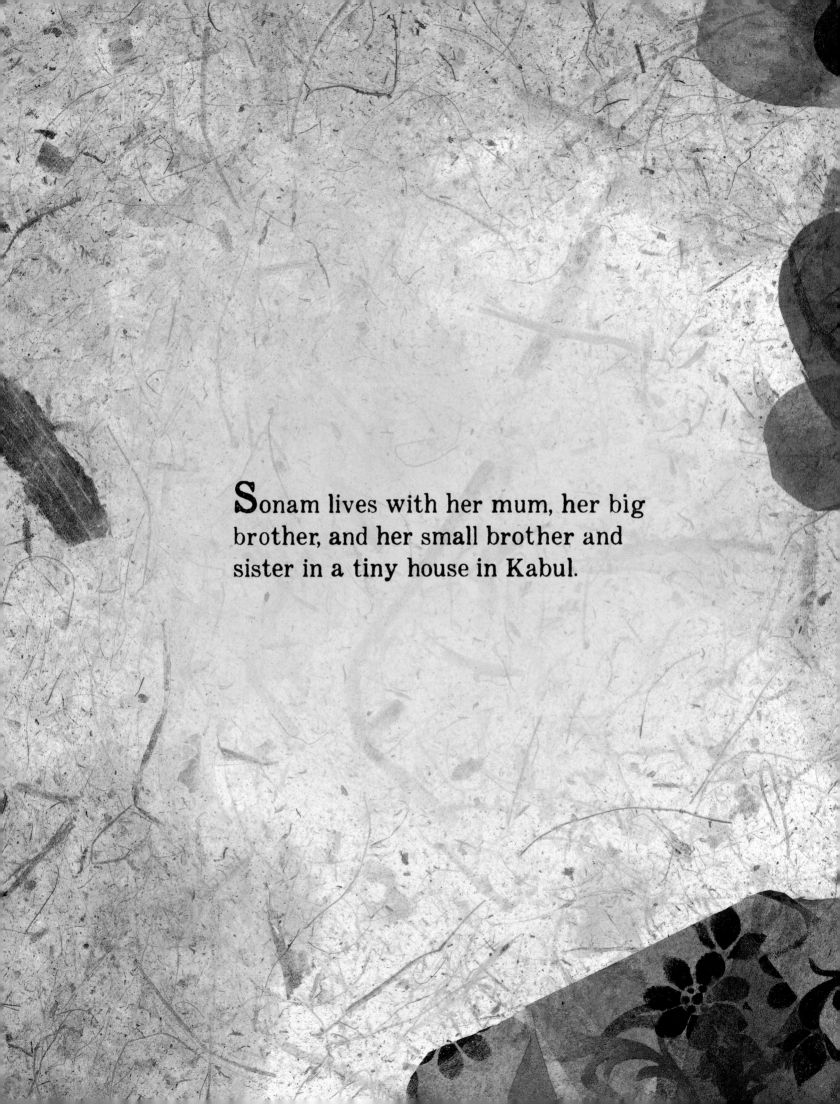

Sonam lives with her mum, her big brother, and her small brother and sister in a tiny house in Kabul.

Sonam's mum sews dresses and shirts, which her big brother sells at the market. Sonam plays hide and seek in the alleyways.

Sonam turns seven and she is no longer a child. Her big brother orders her to cover her hair and begin to work.

Sonam runs into the market. All the noise of the metal beaters, food sellers and beggars makes a storm in her head.

As Sonam runs,
her hair flows in the wind.

And as she runs, Sonam hears a sound
that seems to come from the trees, from the
earth, from her heart. A whisper. She follows
the sound to a garden of mulberry
and pomegranate trees.

Sitting by an open window is an old man.
His eyes are milky and his spine is curved.
He cradles something in his lap.

'Assalaamu Alaykum,' Sonam says quietly. 'What are you doing?'

'Wa-Alaykum Salaam.' The old man smiles. 'I am doing what I've done every day for nearly all my life. I am making music.'

Music. This is what nobody in her country is allowed to hear! This sound, which makes Sonam feel she is both up amongst the stars and deeper than the tree roots, this is music.

'There is music everywhere,' the old man says. 'In the wind, in the earth, in the trees. Music is forbidden, but that's when we need it most. But you can only hear music if you listen with all your heart.'

He holds out his instrument.
'Come, child. Come and play.'

Sonam sneaks away every day to the old man's garden. She learns that music is like a pomegranate tree. It needs nurturing and love to thrive and give fruit.

The old man gives Sonam her own instrument, a rubab, the one he played as a child. It is carved from a single piece of mulberry wood.

Sonam sells chewing gum to people in their cars in the city. She hums her music amongst the shrill car horns and distant gunfire from the mountains. Now she cannot hear these sounds of fear.

One day, her brother hears her humming.
'Where did you learn this?' he asks.

Sonam is afraid, but she tells him about the old man and the music. He takes her rubab and forbids Sonam to play or sing again.

Sonam becomes withdrawn. Her spirit is dull and tired. Her world is so noisy, but it feels so silent. The music drifts away like clouds.

And then there are planes in the sky and the roar of gunfire and rockets. Sonam sees foreign soldiers in goggles and hears a sound she has never heard before. Like music, but angry and electric.

Sonam's music stays silent.

Sonam cannot bear the silence anymore. She goes to the old man's garden, but he has gone and the pomegranate trees have withered.

There is only a single fruit, up high. Sonam picks it and puts the seeds in her pocket.

Sonam will plant the pomegranate seeds in her garden. In time, she will have her own tree.

As she digs, she hits something hard. A wooden box, buried deep in the hard earth. Sonam opens it. Inside is her rubab. Her brother has kept it safe for her.

Now the music floats into Sonam's mind, but it is still broken. She cradles the rubab and feels the rough strings that make such beautiful music.

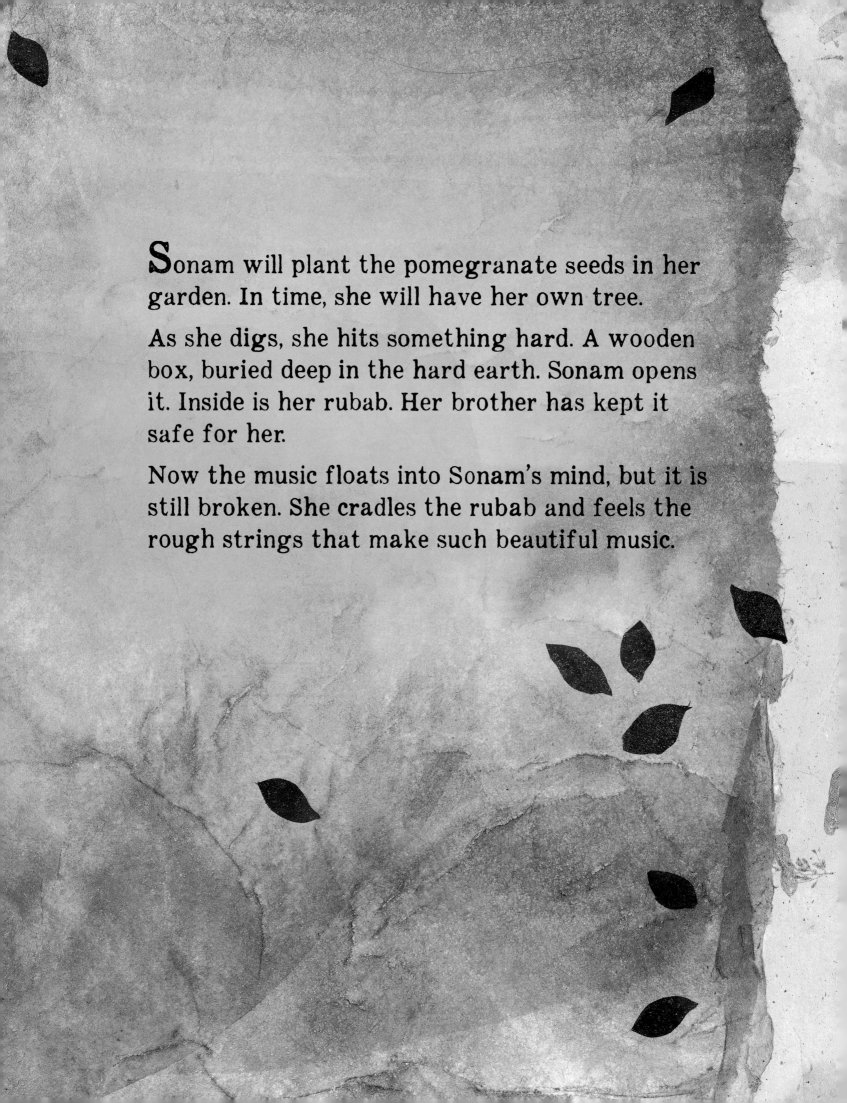

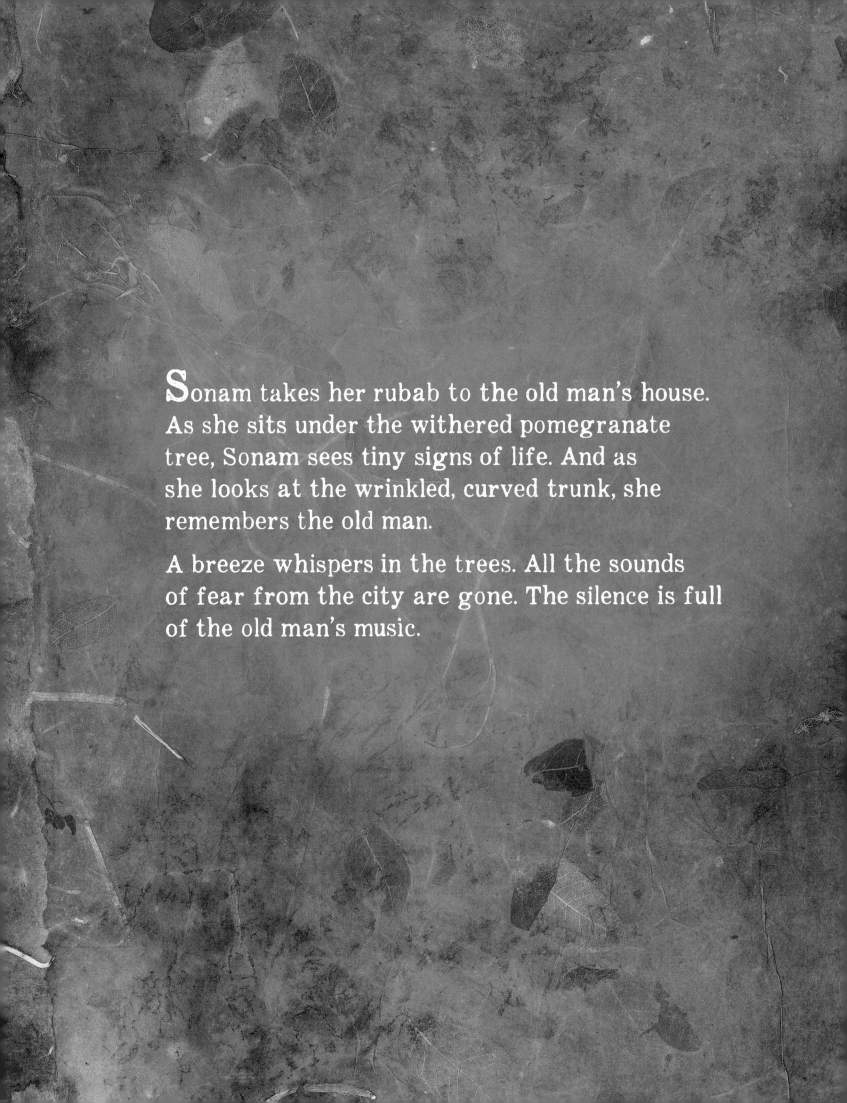

Sonam takes her rubab to the old man's house. As she sits under the withered pomegranate tree, Sonam sees tiny signs of life. And as she looks at the wrinkled, curved trunk, she remembers the old man.

A breeze whispers in the trees. All the sounds of fear from the city are gone. The silence is full of the old man's music.

His music is so clear that she can see it. It is red and bright blue, and sometimes a pale, soft green. It brushes her skin and strokes her hair.

And as it flows back into her, she realises the old man is with her now and always will be. And so will the music.

Because Sonam's heart is opening,
and the music is there inside.

AUTHOR'S NOTE

Music in Afghanistan goes back thousands of years and has influenced music throughout the world. Just think, without the rubab, we wouldn't have the violin! When the Taliban took power in 1996 and banned music of any kind, it was devastating, because Afghans love music like no other people I have ever met. Afghanistan is made up of many different peoples, and music was often the only thing to unite them. A world of silence is so hard to imagine, isn't it? Maybe you can try it, for an hour — perhaps one way to think about it is to imagine sport being banned in Australia. No running, no catching, no swimming, no cheering...

After six years of silence, music was eventually allowed again, and the Afghanistan National Institute of Music was founded by Dr Ahmad Sarmast, an Afghan-Australian. The school took in orphans and children who worked on the street to help their families earn enough money to eat. I worked at the Institute for a year, and the students were some of the hardest-working children I have ever kno wn. One of my students was named Sonam, and she is the inspiration for this book. Before the Institute opened, Sonam had sold chewing gum on the streets of Kabul, but by the time I met her, she had learnt to play the viola, read music and speak English. She was a little older than the Sonam in this story, but I reckon that the Sonam you have just met is about to go to Dr Sarmast's music school.

Anyway, the real Sonam, the one I knew, left the school at eighteen and married to a policeman. I like to think she plays music to her children, and that there will never again be silence in Afghanistan.

Eddie Ayres